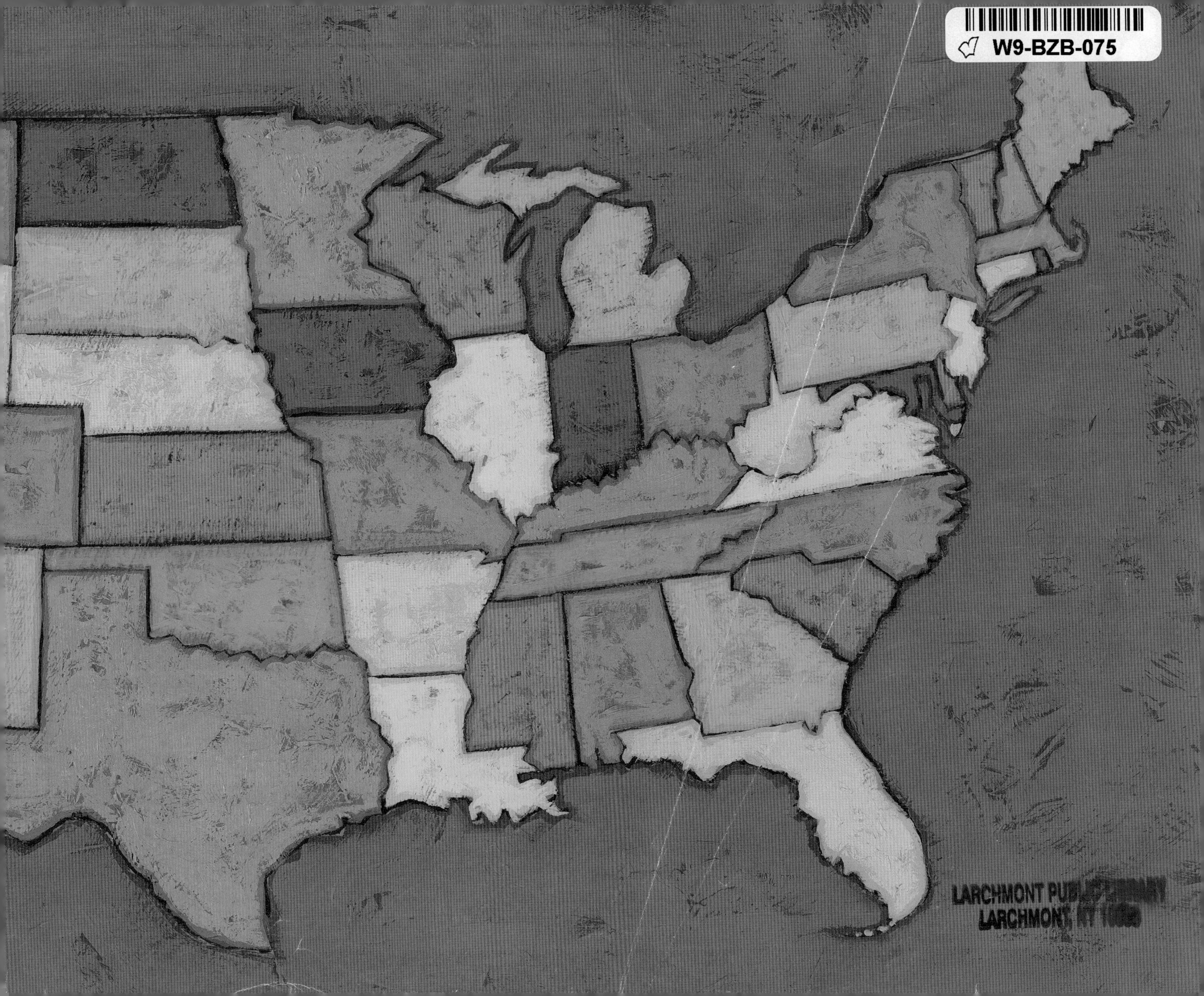

Searching for
Oliver K. Woodman

Searching for

Harcourt, Inc.

Orlando Austin New York San Diego Toronto London

Oliver K. Woodman

Written by DARCY PATTISON

Illustrated by JOE CEPEDA

www.HarcourtBooks.com

Library of Congress Cataloging-in-Publication Data
Pattison, Darcy.
Searching for Oliver K. Woodman/written by Darcy Pattison;
illustrated by Joe Cepeda.
p. cm.
Sequel to: Journey of Oliver K. Woodman.
Summary: Imogene Poplar, a private investigator made of wood, is sent by a reporter and Tameka's Uncle Ray in search of the missing Oliver K. Woodman, and her journey is related through the letters and postcards of those she meets along the way.
[1. Dolls—Fiction. 2. Missing persons—Fiction.
3. Travel—Fiction. 4. Letters—Fiction.
5. Postcards—Fiction.] I. Cepeda, Joe, ill. II. Title.
PZ7.P27816Se 2005
[E]—dc22 2003021447
ISBN 0-15-205184-8

First edition
H G F E D C B A

Manufactured in China

The paintings in this book were done in oils over an acrylic under-painting on board.
The display type was set in Kaufman and Publicity Gothic.
Color separations by Colourscan Co. Pte. Ltd., Singapore
Manufactured by South China Printing Company, Ltd., China
This book was printed on totally chlorine-free Stora Enso Matte paper.
Production supervision by Pascha Gerlinger
Designed by Lydia D'moch

For my friends and family
(who'll find their special dates in Imogene's story)
and with thanks to Amy for walking and talking
—D. P.

For J. M. F. C.
and all your future flights of fancy
—J. C.

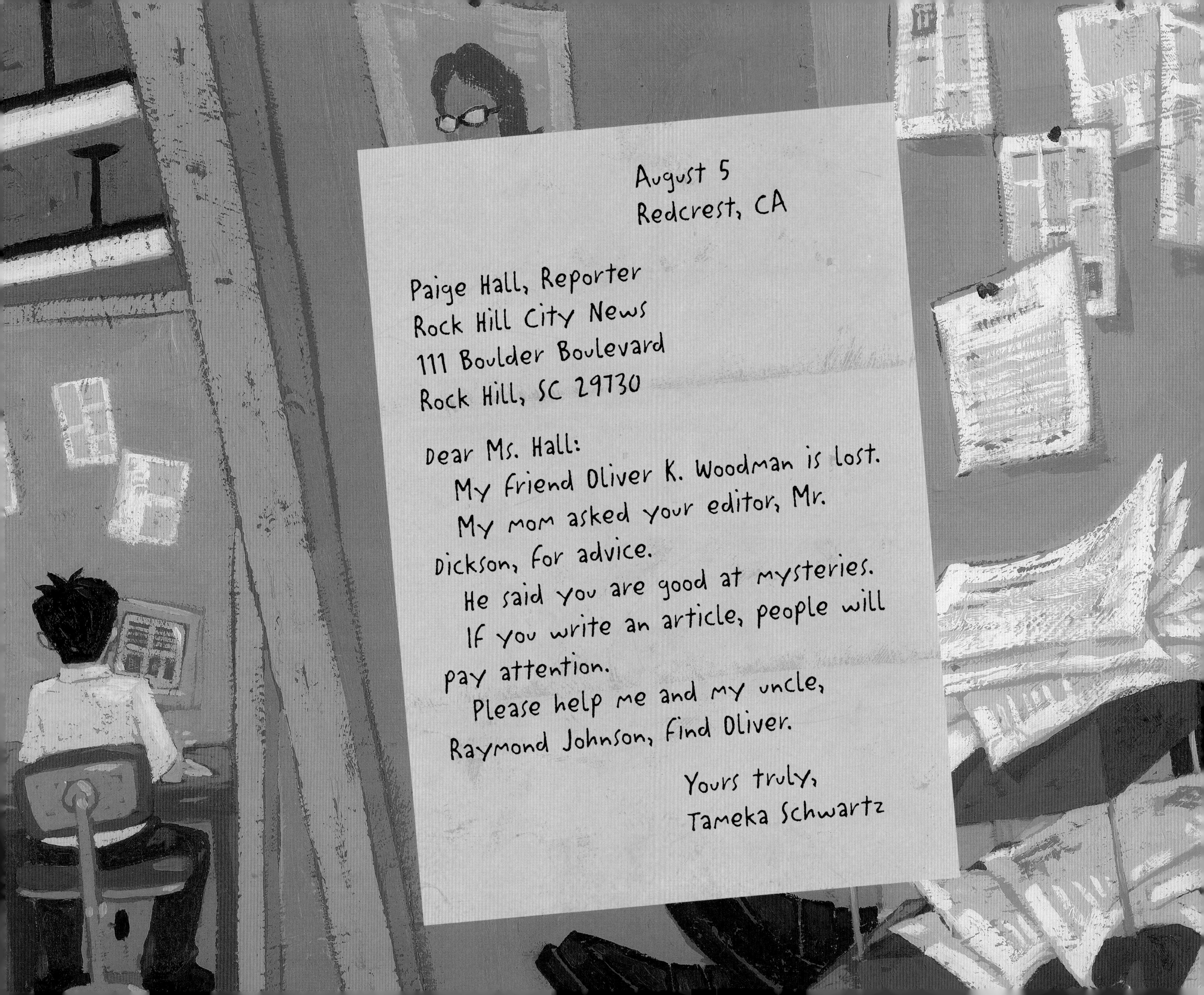

August 5
Redcrest, CA

Paige Hall, Reporter
Rock Hill City News
111 Boulder Boulevard
Rock Hill, SC 29730

Dear Ms. Hall:

My friend Oliver K. Woodman is lost.

My mom asked your editor, Mr. Dickson, for advice.

He said you are good at mysteries.

If you write an article, people will pay attention.

Please help me and my uncle, Raymond Johnson, find Oliver.

Yours truly,
Tameka Schwartz

ROCK HILL CITY NEWS
AUGUST 14

Hometown Boy Lost

by Paige Hall

Mr. Oliver K. Woodman, a local traveler of some renown, has been missing for over sixty days. Last year, he made a historic cross-country journey from Rock Hill, South Carolina, to Redcrest, California. He was trying to repeat the journey this summer. He left on June 1. Since then, no one has heard from Mr. Woodman.

"Oliver knows how to take care of himself," says Rock Hill resident Mr. Raymond Johnson. "But it's been so long that I'm starting to worry."

Mr. Woodman was last seen wearing a hat and a backpack. If you have seen Mr. Woodman, or have any information as to his whereabouts, contact this newspaper.

September 1
Rock Hill, SC

Dear Tameka:

Oliver is still lost. Your Uncle Ray is very upset.

We have decided to send out a private investigator to find Oliver.

Cross your fingers!

Paige Hall,
Reporter

P.S. Your uncle is quite charming!

Dear Traveler,

I am a private investigator searching for Mr. Oliver K. Woodman. He was last seen on June 1 near Rock Hill, South Carolina. Please help me find him. If you don't mind, drop a note to my friend Paige Hall, 111 Boulder Boulevard, Rock Hill, South Carolina 29730. She wants to keep up with my investigation.

Thanks,

MS. IMOGENE POPLAR, P.I.

September 15
New York City, NY

My Dearest Paige:

I was visiting my sick aunt in South Carolina when I saw Ms. Imogene's sign. To help, I brought her north to search for Oliver. Alas! I caught a cold from my aunt. My voice has been perfectly dreadful for the last three days. Ms. Imogene's quiet ways were a blessing. Now that I'm better, I'll send Ms. Imogene on her way. I hope I haven't delayed her too much . . .

Perhaps not. My leading man told me about a fellow he picked up somewhere down south and left just outside Hershey, Pennsylvania. The man wore a hat, but didn't have a backpack. Could this be your Oliver? The stage manager is on his way to Hershey and will take Ms. Imogene that far.

Gratefully yours,
Bella Maria Lopez,
Voted "The Best Voice on Broadway"

P. S. I've enclosed two tickets to my musical. Ms. Imogene enjoyed it immensely.

GOTHAM
OPERA
CO.
STAGE RT

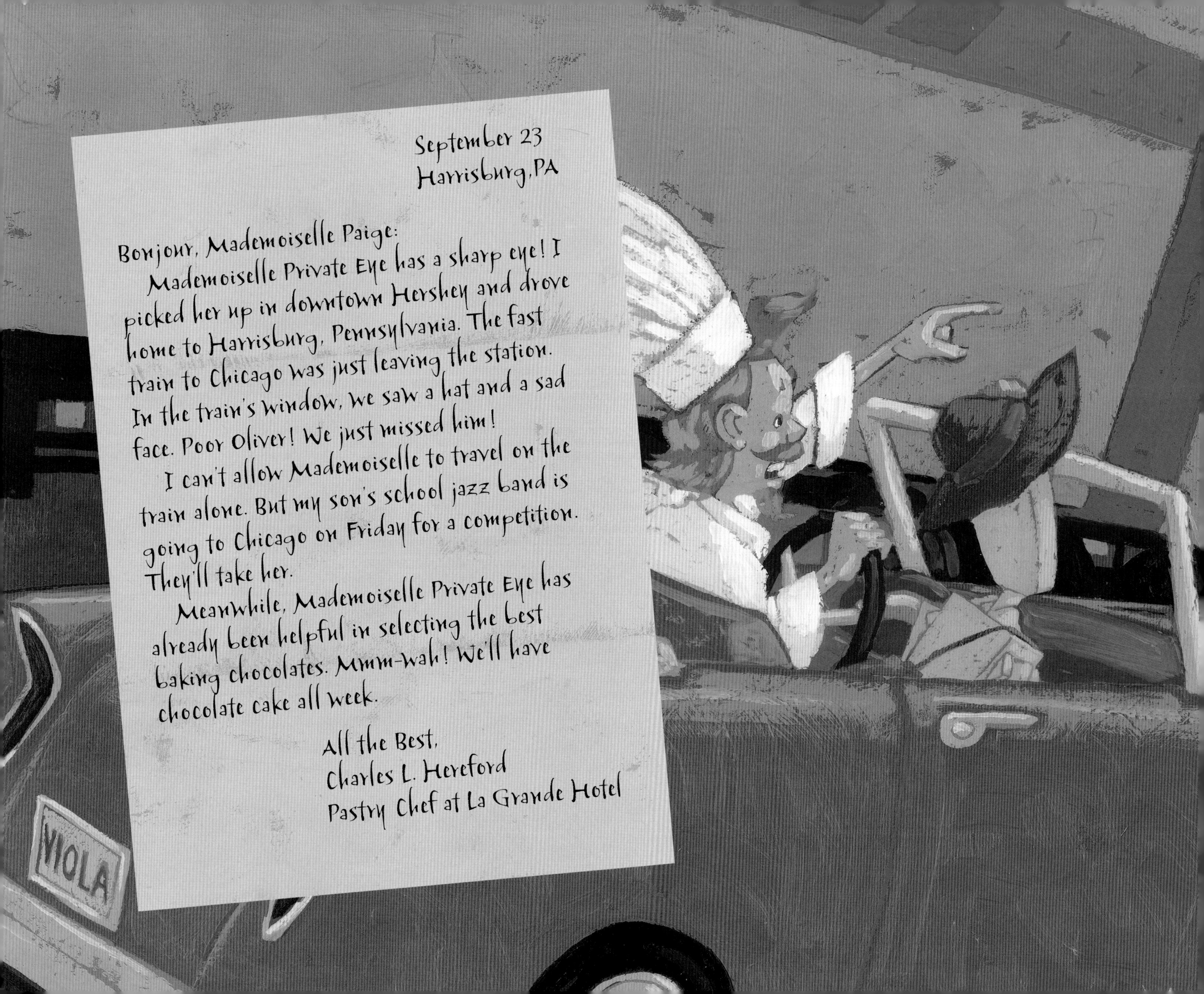

September 23
Harrisburg, PA

Bonjour, Mademoiselle Paige:

Mademoiselle Private Eye has a sharp eye! I picked her up in downtown Hershey and drove home to Harrisburg, Pennsylvania. The fast train to Chicago was just leaving the station. In the train's window, we saw a hat and a sad face. Poor Oliver! We just missed him!

I can't allow Mademoiselle to travel on the train alone. But my son's school jazz band is going to Chicago on Friday for a competition. They'll take her.

Meanwhile, Mademoiselle Private Eye has already been helpful in selecting the best baking chocolates. Mmm-wah! We'll have chocolate cake all week.

All the Best,
Charles L. Hereford
Pastry Chef at La Grande Hotel

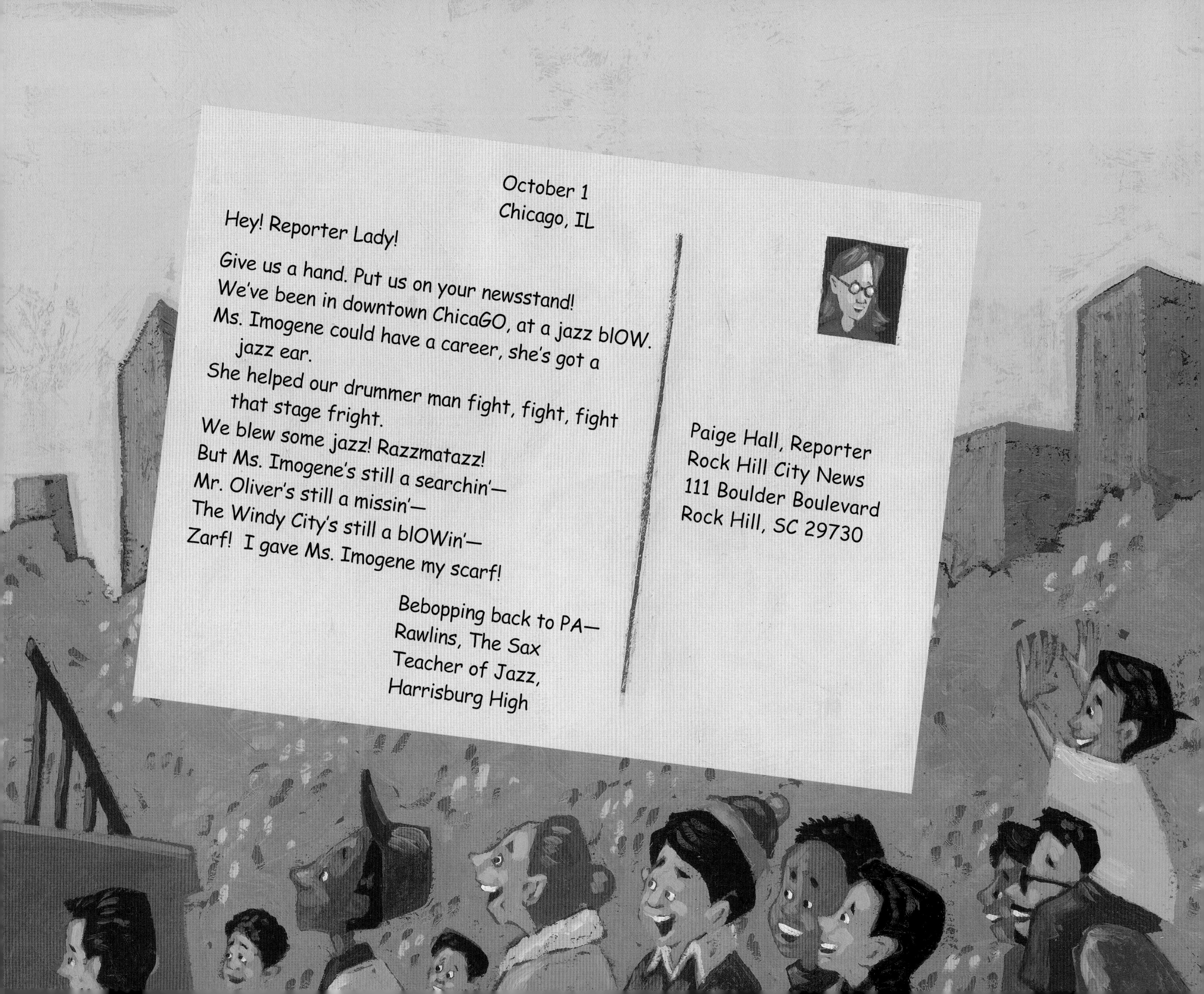
October 1
Chicago, IL

Hey! Reporter Lady!

Give us a hand. Put us on your newsstand!
We've been in downtown ChicaGO, at a jazz blOW.
Ms. Imogene could have a career, she's got a
jazz ear.
She helped our drummer man fight, fight, fight
that stage fright.
We blew some jazz! Razzmatazz!
But Ms. Imogene's still a searchin'—
Mr. Oliver's still a missin'—
The Windy City's still a blOWin'—
Zarf! I gave Ms. Imogene my scarf!

Bebopping back to PA—
Rawlins, The Sax
Teacher of Jazz,
Harrisburg High

Paige Hall, Reporter
Rock Hill City News
111 Boulder Boulevard
Rock Hill, SC 29730

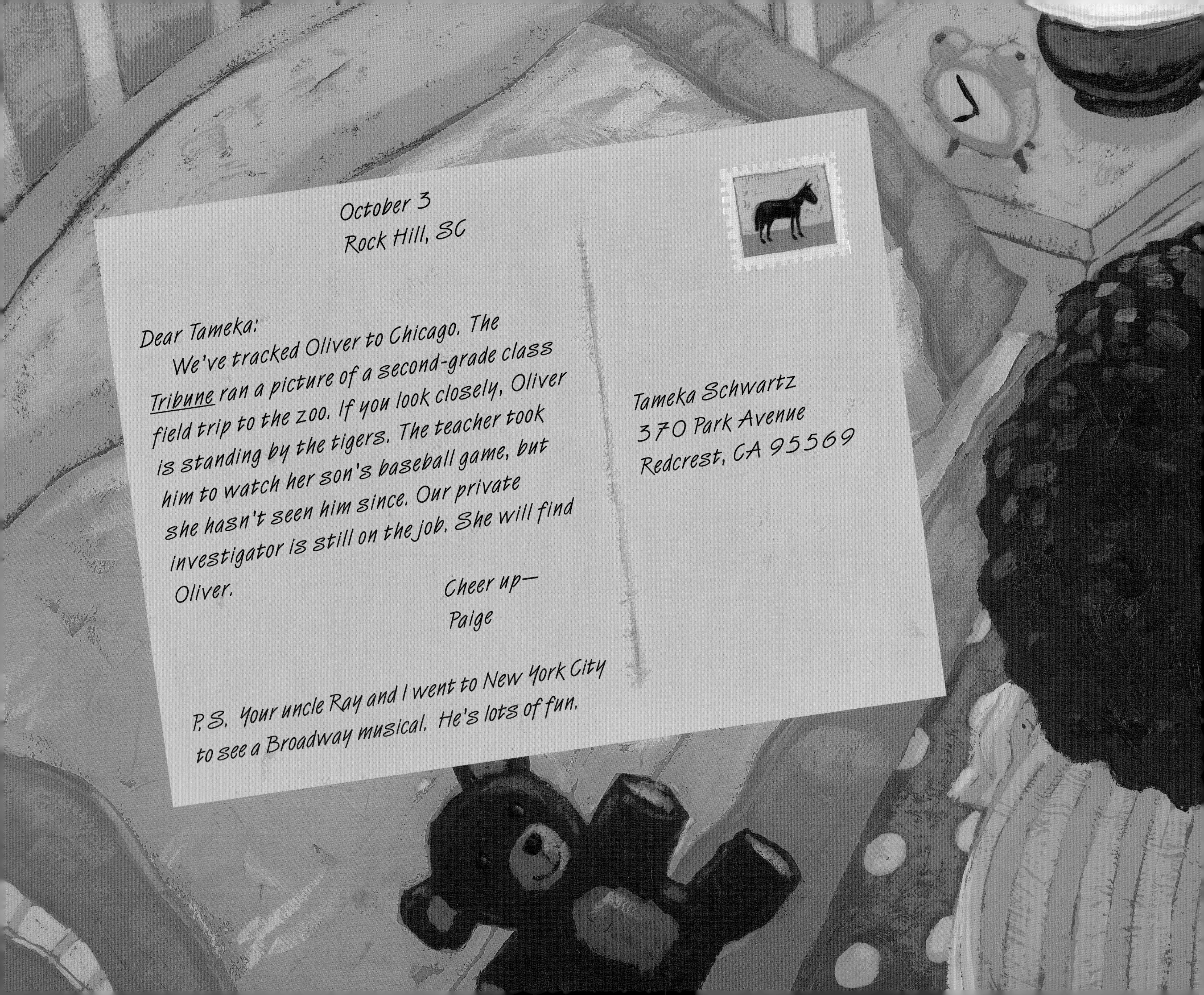
October 3
Rock Hill, SC

Dear Tameka:
We've tracked Oliver to Chicago. The Tribune ran a picture of a second-grade class field trip to the zoo. If you look closely, Oliver is standing by the tigers. The teacher took him to watch her son's baseball game, but she hasn't seen him since. Our private investigator is still on the job. She will find Oliver.

Cheer up—
Paige

P.S. Your uncle Ray and I went to New York City to see a Broadway musical. He's lots of fun.

Tameka Schwartz
370 Park Avenue
Redcrest, CA 95569

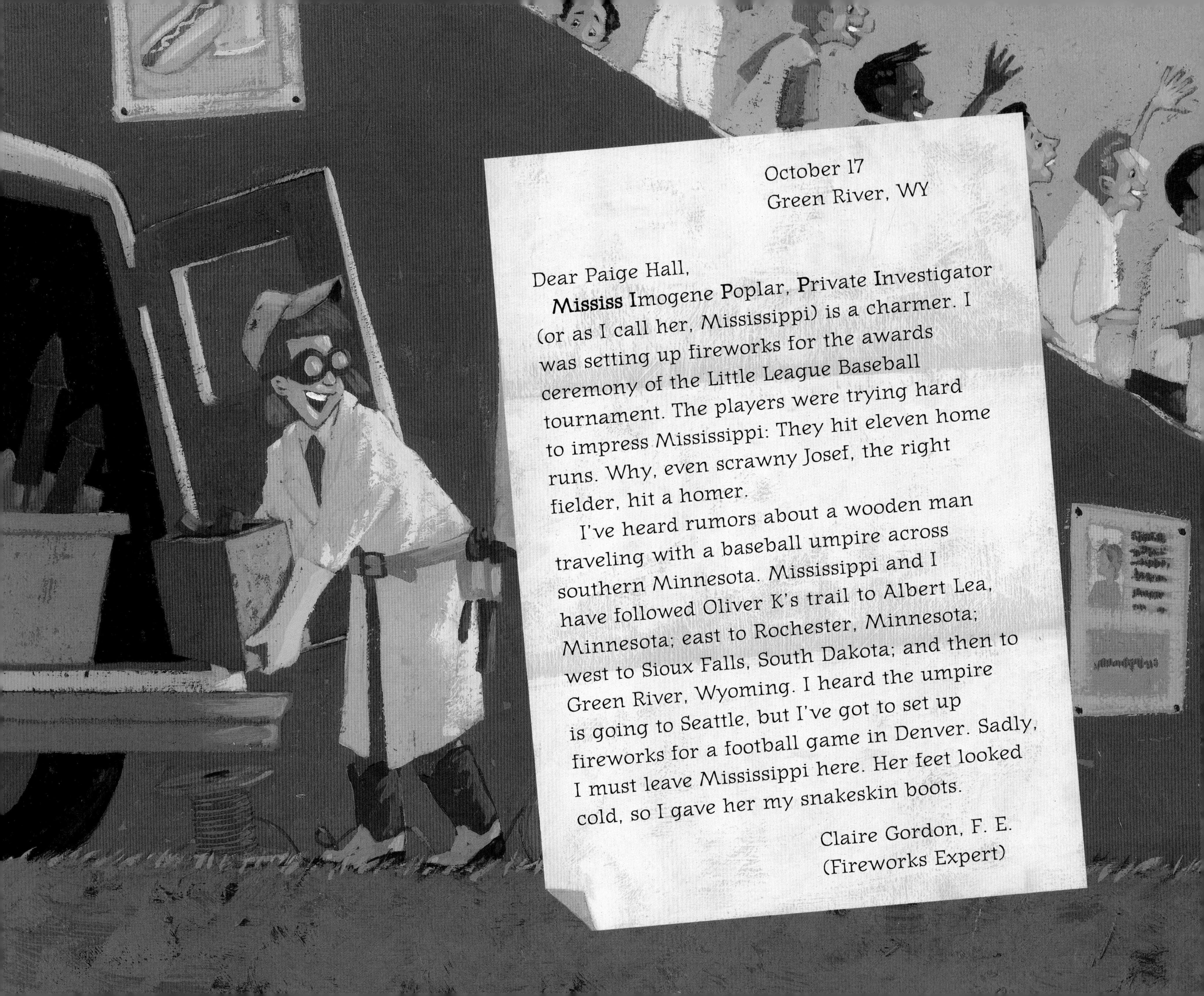
October 17
Green River, WY

Dear Paige Hall,

Mississ **I**mogene **P**oplar, **P**rivate **I**nvestigator (or as I call her, Mississippi) is a charmer. I was setting up fireworks for the awards ceremony of the Little League Baseball tournament. The players were trying hard to impress Mississippi: They hit eleven home runs. Why, even scrawny Josef, the right fielder, hit a homer.

I've heard rumors about a wooden man traveling with a baseball umpire across southern Minnesota. Mississippi and I have followed Oliver K's trail to Albert Lea, Minnesota; east to Rochester, Minnesota; west to Sioux Falls, South Dakota; and then to Green River, Wyoming. I heard the umpire is going to Seattle, but I've got to set up fireworks for a football game in Denver. Sadly, I must leave Mississippi here. Her feet looked cold, so I gave her my snakeskin boots.

Claire Gordon, F. E.
(Fireworks Expert)

EEEHA

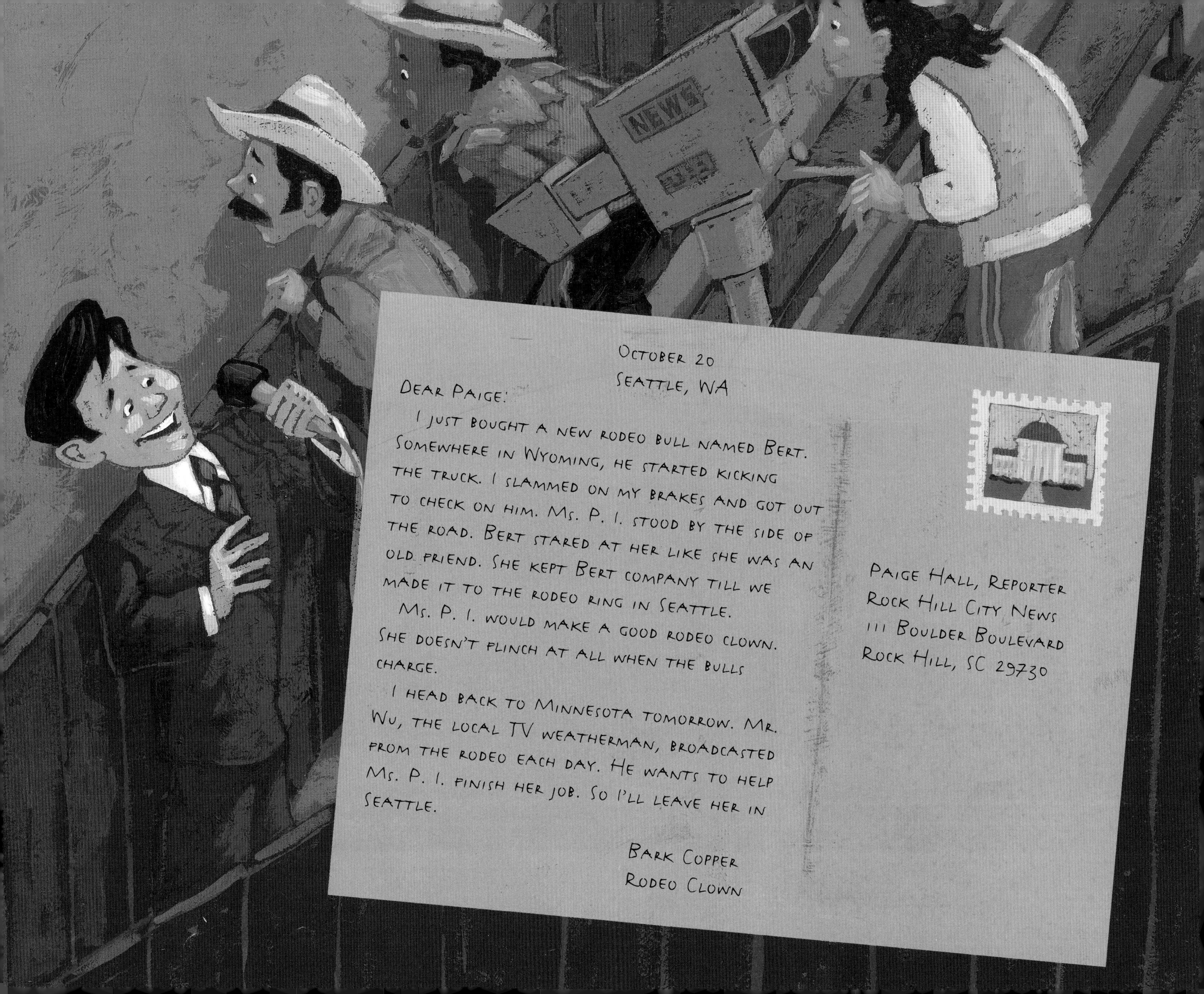

OCTOBER 20
SEATTLE, WA

DEAR PAIGE:

I JUST BOUGHT A NEW RODEO BULL NAMED BERT. SOMEWHERE IN WYOMING, HE STARTED KICKING THE TRUCK. I SLAMMED ON MY BRAKES AND GOT OUT TO CHECK ON HIM. MS. P. I. STOOD BY THE SIDE OF THE ROAD. BERT STARED AT HER LIKE SHE WAS AN OLD FRIEND. SHE KEPT BERT COMPANY TILL WE MADE IT TO THE RODEO RING IN SEATTLE.

MS. P. I. WOULD MAKE A GOOD RODEO CLOWN. SHE DOESN'T FLINCH AT ALL WHEN THE BULLS CHARGE.

I HEAD BACK TO MINNESOTA TOMORROW. MR. WU, THE LOCAL TV WEATHERMAN, BROADCASTED FROM THE RODEO EACH DAY. HE WANTS TO HELP MS. P. I. FINISH HER JOB. SO I'LL LEAVE HER IN SEATTLE.

BARK COPPER
RODEO CLOWN

PAIGE HALL, REPORTER
ROCK HILL CITY NEWS
111 BOULDER BOULEVARD
ROCK HILL, SC 29730

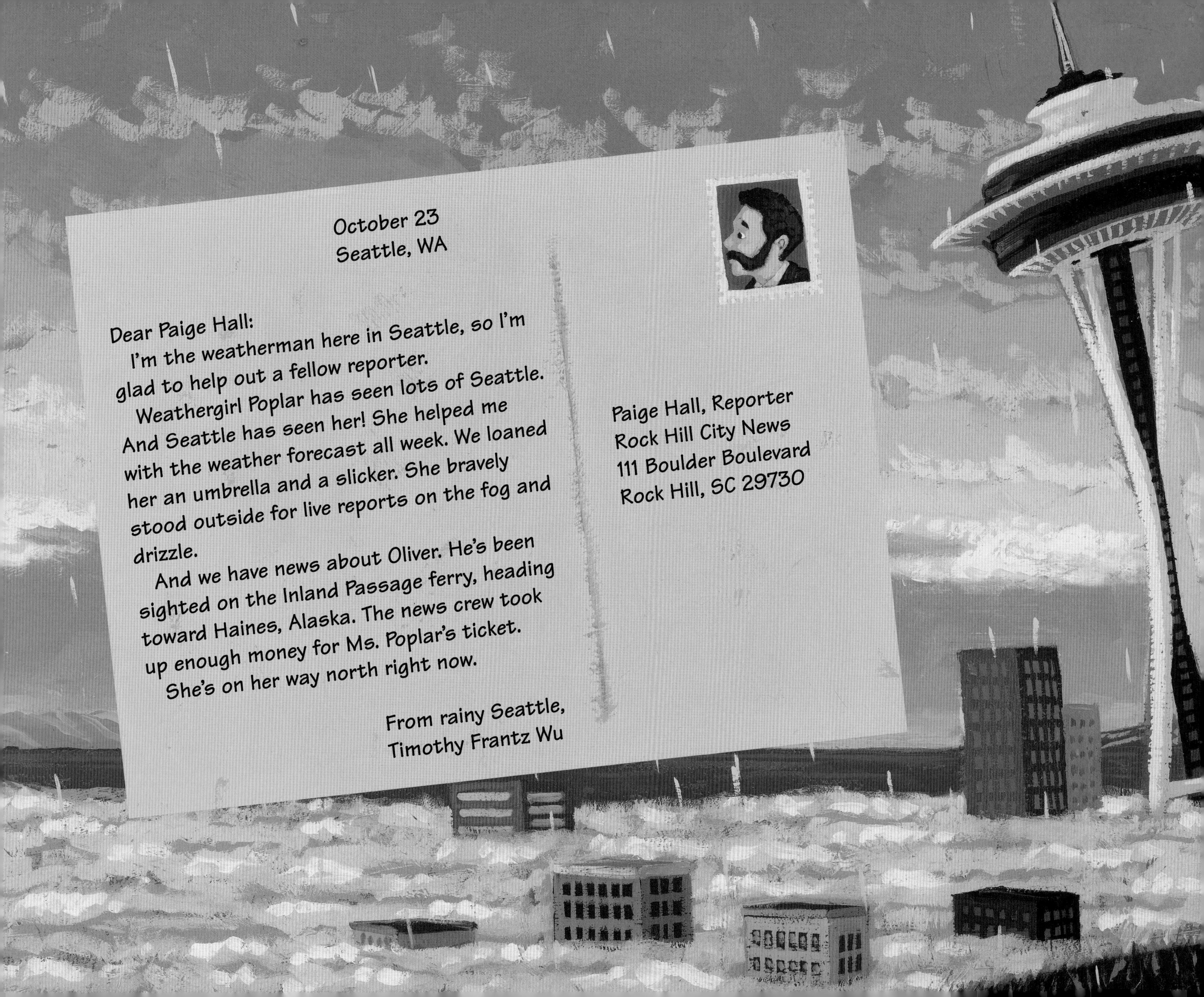
October 23
Seattle, WA
Dear Paige Hall:
I'm the weatherman here in Seattle, so I'm glad to help out a fellow reporter.
Weathergirl Poplar has seen lots of Seattle. And Seattle has seen her! She helped me with the weather forecast all week. We loaned her an umbrella and a slicker. She bravely stood outside for live reports on the fog and drizzle.
And we have news about Oliver. He's been sighted on the Inland Passage ferry, heading toward Haines, Alaska. The news crew took up enough money for Ms. Poplar's ticket. She's on her way north right now.
From rainy Seattle,
Timothy Frantz Wu
Paige Hall, Reporter
Rock Hill City News
111 Boulder Boulevard
Rock Hill, SC 29730

October 31
Redcrest, CA

Dear Paige:

Boo! Happy Halloween.

Mama was excited when Uncle Ray called and said he's bringing you to see us. She wants to meet her baby brother's new friend.

We can go fishing if you want.

Oliver liked fishing. Where, oh where, is Oliver? Alaska is so big and so far away.

Love,
Tameka
XOXO

P. S. Knock, knock. Who's there? Boo. Boo who? I'm crying about Oliver, too!

November 1
Eagle River, AK

Dear Reporter Paige—

Hi, I'm Jake. Hi, I'm Amy. We're twins! Today mr. Ollie helped us snowboard.

Mr. Ollie taught me (Jake) to keep on trying.

Mr. Ollie taught me (Amy) to be brave.

Later we met Ms. Imogene Poplar. Guess what? She was looking for Mr. Ollie. But he was gone! We heard that a snowboarder flew him to Barrow, Alaska. Tomorrow our friend Mr. George Qiruk will fly Ms. Imogene to the Top of the World. Don't worry—the trail is hot.

Be brave!

Jake and Amy Bisson

P. S. Ms. Imogene loves bedtime stories.

November 5
Top of the World
Barrow, AK

Dear Paige Hall:
Yes! Your private investigator finally found your friend! I guess Oliver and Imogene had never met. But they understood each other like they were old friends.
I'm sorry you missed them when you phoned. They were together out on the tundra, watching the northern lights.
I will make sure they are at Ms. Tameka Schwartz's house by November 15. They won't want to miss such a special day.

Sincerely,
George Qiruk

Paige Hall, Reporter
Rock Hill City News
111 Boulder Boulevard
Rock Hill, SC 29730

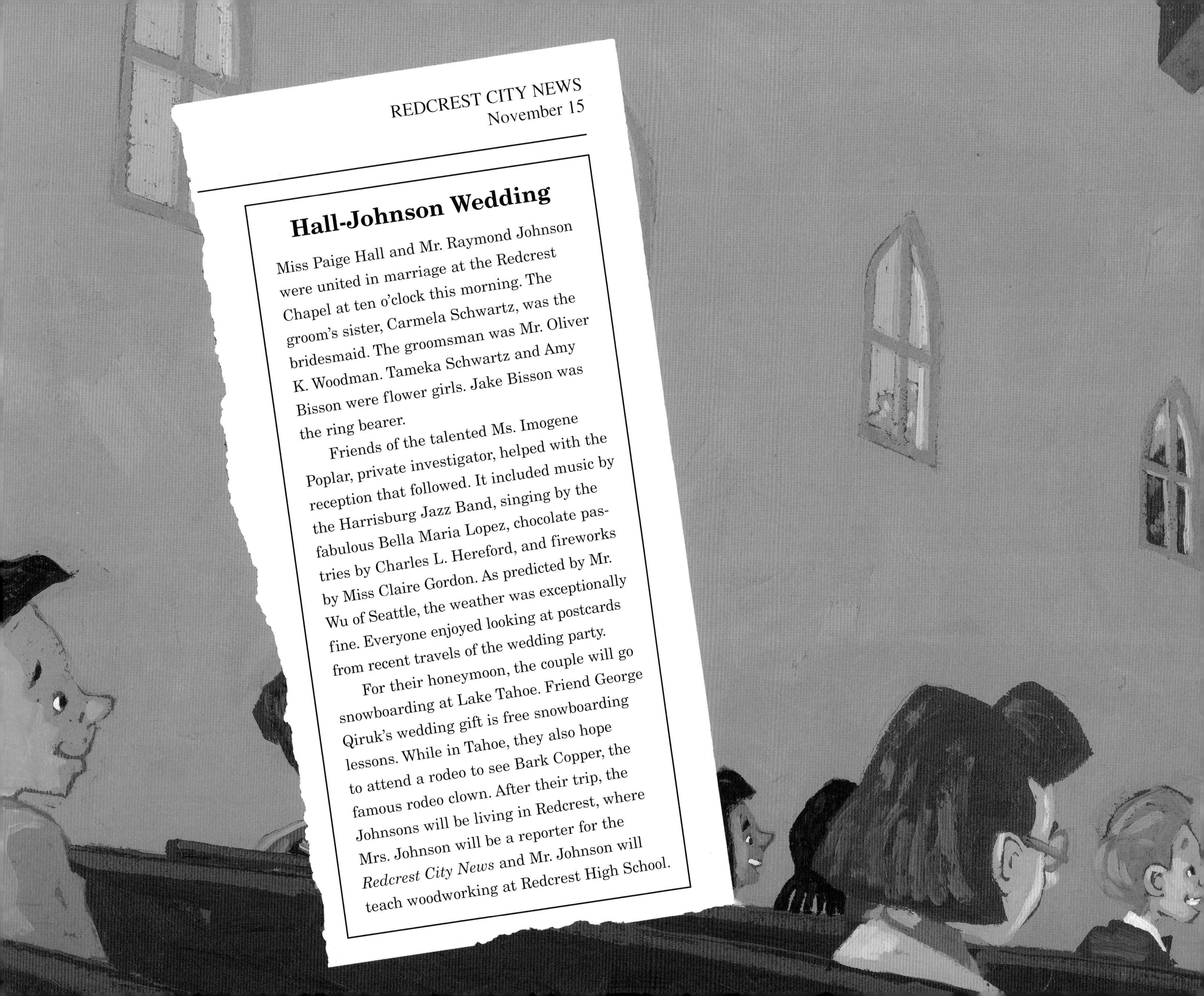

REDCREST CITY NEWS
November 15

Hall-Johnson Wedding

Miss Paige Hall and Mr. Raymond Johnson were united in marriage at the Redcrest Chapel at ten o'clock this morning. The groom's sister, Carmela Schwartz, was the bridesmaid. The groomsman was Mr. Oliver K. Woodman. Tameka Schwartz and Amy Bisson were flower girls. Jake Bisson was the ring bearer.

Friends of the talented Ms. Imogene Poplar, private investigator, helped with the reception that followed. It included music by the Harrisburg Jazz Band, singing by the fabulous Bella Maria Lopez, chocolate pastries by Charles L. Hereford, and fireworks by Miss Claire Gordon. As predicted by Mr. Wu of Seattle, the weather was exceptionally fine. Everyone enjoyed looking at postcards from recent travels of the wedding party.

For their honeymoon, the couple will go snowboarding at Lake Tahoe. Friend George Qiruk's wedding gift is free snowboarding lessons. While in Tahoe, they also hope to attend a rodeo to see Bark Copper, the famous rodeo clown. After their trip, the Johnsons will be living in Redcrest, where Mrs. Johnson will be a reporter for the *Redcrest City News* and Mr. Johnson will teach woodworking at Redcrest High School.

JUST MARRIED
I ♥ WUD

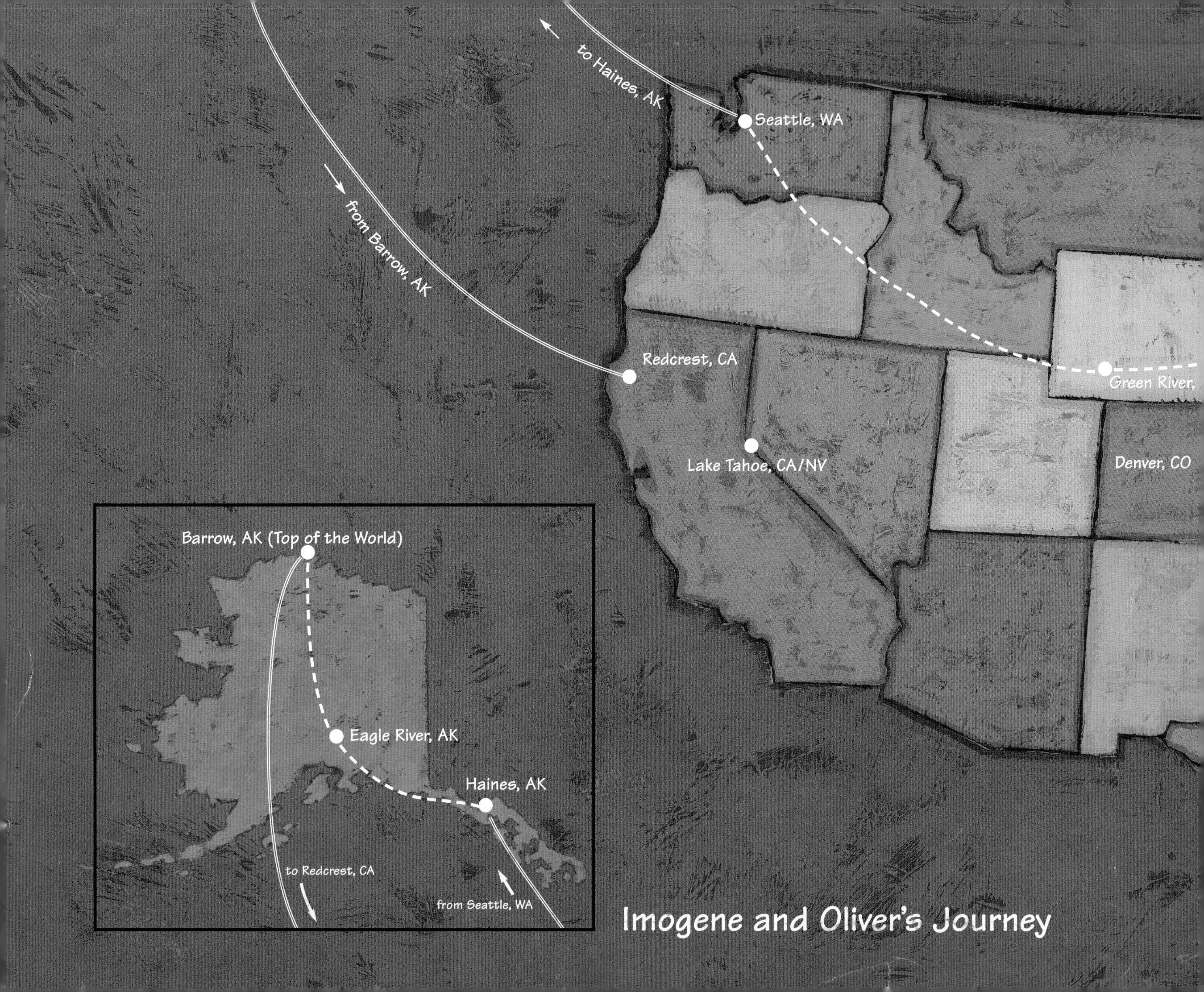

Imogene and Oliver's Journey

to Haines, AK
Seattle, WA
from Barrow, AK
Redcrest, CA
Green River,
Lake Tahoe, CA/NV
Denver, CO
Barrow, AK (Top of the World)
Eagle River, AK
Haines, AK
to Redcrest, CA
from Seattle, WA